D0181383

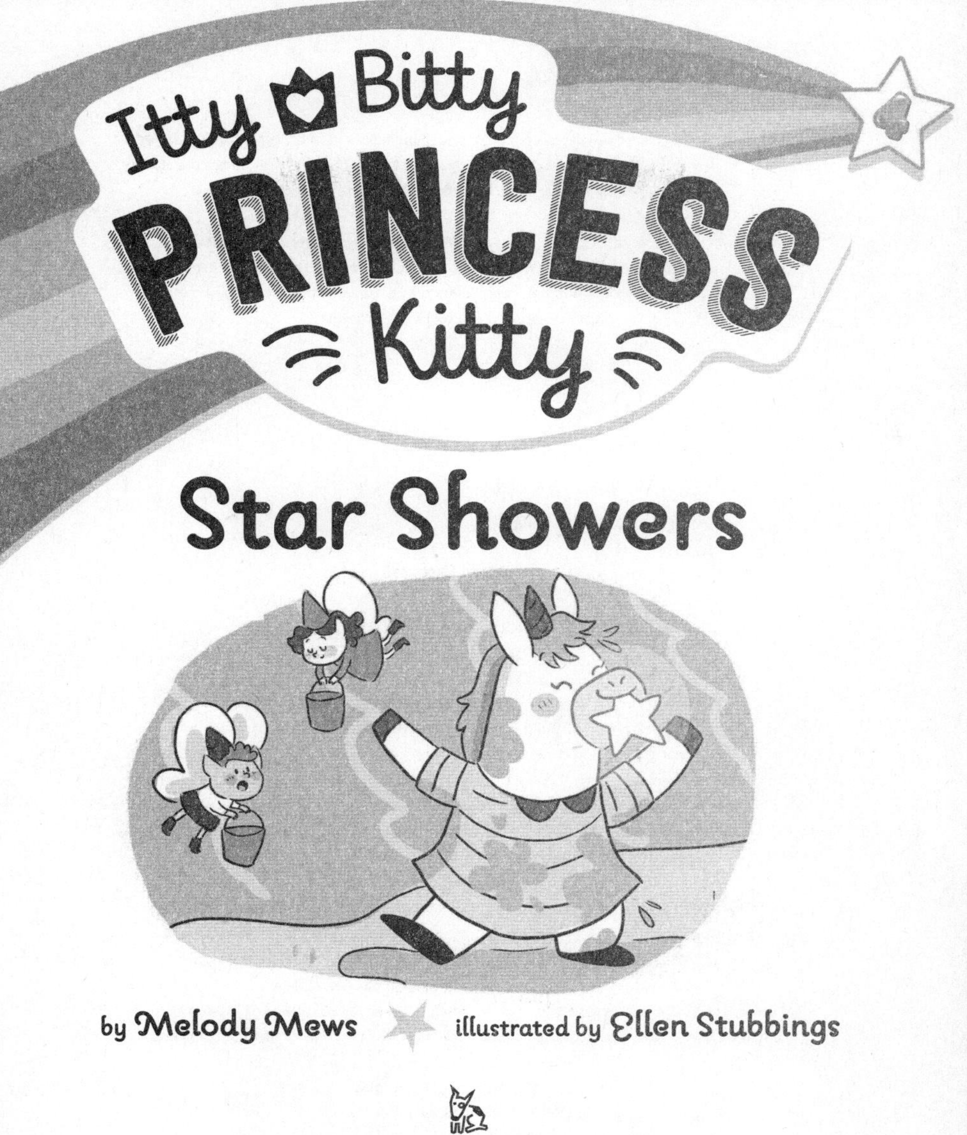

by Melody Mews ★ illustrated by Ellen Stubbings

LITTLE SIMON
New York London Toronto Sydney New Delhi

LITTLE SIMON
An imprint of Simon & Schuster Children's Publishing Division
1230 Avenue of the Americas, New York, New York 10020
First Little Simon paperback edition August 2020.
Designed by Laura Roode. The text of this book was set in Banda.
Manufactured in the United States of America 0620 MTN 10 9 8 7 6 5 4 3 2 1
Cataloging-in-Publication Data is available for this title from the Library of Congress.
ISBN 978-1-5344-6361-5 (hc)
ISBN 978-1-5344-6360-8 (pbk)
ISBN 978-1-5344-6362-2 (eBook)

Contents

chapter 1
Itty's Room

The Missing Tiara

Knock-knock-knock.

Someone was knocking on Itty Bitty Princess Kitty's bedroom door. It was the Queen of Lollyland, also known as Itty's mother.

"I came to remind you to tidy up your closet, but I see you beat me to it!" Queen Kitty said with a smile.

"Almost done!" Itty exclaimed.

"I'll see you soon for breakfast then, darling," the Queen replied.

Even though Itty was the princess of Lollyland, she still had to do chores, like tidying up her closet when it was messy.

And her closet was *definitely* messy after Itty's friend Luna Unicorn left yesterday. The girls had played dress-up, and most of Itty's clothes had landed on the floor. But now everything was back where it belonged.

Something still isn't right, Itty thought. She looked more closely. Her dresses were on hangers, and her shoes were neatly stacked on the shoe rack.

What can it be? Itty wondered. And then she realized exactly what it was. Her tiara. It was gone!

The tiara usually sat on a velvet pillow on the center shelf of her closet. The pillow was there, but the tiara wasn't.

Itty remembered taking the tiara down while playing dress-up. And she remembered Luna handing it back after she wore it. She just couldn't remember where she had put it after that.

Itty felt a pang in her tummy.

Was her tiara truly missing?

chapter 2

Once in a Lifetime

Itty forgot all about her *possibly* missing tiara as she enjoyed a delicious breakfast of fluffy purple pancakes and lollyfruit—a special fruit grown only in Lollyland that was a cross between a pineapple and a peach, with a hint of cinnamon.

KNOCK!
KNOCK!
KNOCK
KNOCK
KNOCK
KNOCK
KNOCK
KNOCK
KNOCK!
KNOCK!

Suddenly, they heard a knock at the palace door. They could hear the knock because there was a special series of tunnels in the walls that allowed the sound to travel so that wherever the Kitty family was, they'd be able to hear someone arriving. The royal architect had designed the palace that way.

Itty wiped her whiskers and followed her parents to the grand entrance hall.

The cats were surprised to see Glenn Groundhog, Lollyland's

royal weather forecaster, at the door. Glenn usually sent in his daily forecast by fairy because he only left his burrow on Groundhog Day . . . but that was months away.

"Pardon the interruption," Glenn said, removing his little red hat and bowing. "But during my scan of the skies this morning, I discovered that there's going to be a star shower tonight!"

"How wonderful!" the King boomed. "We'll alert the kingdom!"

"I'll dispatch the announcement fairies!" the Queen exclaimed.

"What's a star shower?" Itty asked.

"I'll arrange the search," the King replied.

"What's a star shower?" Itty repeated.

"Okay, the fairies have been alerted," the Queen said.

"Mom, how did you alert the fairies already?" Itty was so confused. "And *what* is a star shower?"

"Oh! We forgot this will be your first star shower!" the King said excitedly. "A star shower is an extra-special event that only happens once or twice in a lifetime.

Tonight, thousands of stars will fall from the sky, landing all over Lollyland! And not just any stars," he continued. "These are *wish-granting* stars! Tomorrow we'll hold a star search to give every animal in the kingdom a chance to find a star and make a wish."

"And the wishes all come true?" Itty asked.

Her father nodded. "As long as you don't tell anyone what you wished for."

"*Every* animal who finds a star gets a wish that's guaranteed to come true?!" Itty shouted as she danced around in excitement. "I can't wait to tell my friends!"

"You don't have to wait!" the Queen replied. "The fairies have notified everyone to gather here for a royal announcement. All animals of the kingdom should be arriving any minute now."

And at that very moment, Itty heard a commotion outside.

chapter 3

The King's Announcement

Itty peered down from the balcony. Just as her mom had said, the entire kingdom was assembled and waiting.

As she scanned the crowd, Itty saw flocks of flamingos, caravans of camels, and even prickles of porcupines. Finally, a burst of colorful glitter caught Itty's eye, and she spotted Luna. Luna's horn spouted glitter whenever she was excited, and she was

understandably *very* excited right now! Next to Luna, and covered in glitter, were Itty's other best friends, Chipper Bunny and Esme Butterfly.

Itty waved to her friends. Luna pointed to her head and mouthed something. But Itty couldn't figure out what Luna was trying to say. Then she suddenly understood. Luna was asking Itty where her tiara was.

Itty felt another pang in her tummy. She had actually forgotten about the tiara until she'd gone to change for the royal announcement. And now it felt strange to be standing on the balcony dressed in a princess gown, but without her tiara.

Would *all* of Lollyland notice she wasn't wearing it?

King Kitty stepped to the front of the balcony. A hush fell over the crowd.

Itty listened as the King told the animals about the upcoming star shower and how they would all have a chance to make a wish that was *guaranteed* to come true.

Itty already knew exactly what she was going to wish for if she found a star. She was going to wish to have her tiara back.

That evening, Itty was back on the balcony with her parents. After the announcement, she had continued to search for her tiara. But she hadn't found it.

Out on the balcony this time, there was no crowd gathered below. All the animals of Lollyland were at home, waiting for the star shower.

"I think it's beginning," the Queen murmured.

Itty looked up. The night sky shimmered like a sea of jewels. Moments later, there was a blast of light. Colors swirled in the sky, and then finally the stars began to fall.

Whoa, Itty breathed as she watched the star shower. It reminded her of when her shooting star had arrived—the shooting star that had made her Princess of Lollyland.

But unlike her shooting star,

which had come right to her, these stars fell slowly and scattered everywhere. Itty tried to see where they landed, but it was impossible to tell.

For a moment Lollyland was covered in a blanket of stars. Then, all at once, the stars dimmed. The night was dark again. The stars were hidden, waiting to be discovered and wished upon.

chapter 4

Ready, Set, Star Search!

When Itty woke up the next morning, she thought about how beautiful last night's star shower had been. But now that the star shower was over, that meant . . .

It was time for the star *search*!

Itty leaped out of bed and ran

to her closet to get dressed. Her eyes drifted to the empty pillow on the center shelf.

I really need to find a star so my wish can come true, Itty thought.

A few moments later she hurried downstairs to say goodbye to her parents.

"I'm meeting my friends at Goodie Grove for the star search," Itty called.

"Good luck," the Queen replied.

"Don't forget to eat breakfast there!"

"I won't!" Itty said as she ran out the door. Luckily, a cloud pulled up moments later.

"To Goodie Grove!" Itty cried. "The faster the better!"

Although as Itty's speedy cloud raced across the sky, Itty sort of regretted commanding it to go so fast.

“Are you okay?” Esme asked when Itty landed at Goodie Grove.

“You look kind of green,” said Luna, as she munched on a waffle on a stick.

"Just a little cloud-sick," Itty said, managing a smile. "I'll be fine in a second."

"Who's ready to start STAR SEARCHING?!" Luna shouted, glitter flying everywhere.

Itty grinned and took a bite of her waffle. She was feeling better now. "Let's do this!" she cried.

As Itty and her friends began their search, they realized how crowded the grove was.

"It looks like half of Lollyland came here to look for stars," Chipper commented. Then he turned his attention to something else. "Hey, does that lemon drop bush look like it's glowing? I wonder if . . ." Suddenly Chipper darted into the bush.

chapter 5

Itty Misses Out?

Moments later, Chipper hopped out, cradling a star in his hands.

"Found one!" he cried.

"Way to go, Chipper!" Itty cheered.

"I see one!" Esme exclaimed, flitting toward a candy apple tree.

Itty held her breath until Esme returned, clutching a beautiful star.

Next Luna shrieked and galloped to the syrup river. She dove in horn first and quickly emerged, dripping in syrup and holding a star in her mouth. She scurried away before the syrup fairies yelled at her.

All around the grove, animals were finding stars. Itty was happy for everyone. But as more stars were found, she began to worry: What if she couldn't find one?

Itty drifted away from her friends and leaned against a tree. She didn't want them to see how disappointed she was. Not when they had so much to be excited about. After all, *their* wishes would come true.

As Itty rested, she felt something bop her on the head. Were buttercones falling from the tree? She reached up to remove whatever was nestled in her fur.

It didn't *feel* like a buttercone.

And it didn't *look* like a buttercone. It looked like . . . a shimmering star!

chapter 6

Make a Wish!

"So the stars just float back up?" Itty asked for the fourth time.

"Yes," her mom replied. "You'll close your eyes, make a wish, and then release your star. When it's time, that is."

Itty nodded and closed her eyes.

Finally the mermaids sang their nine notes, indicating that it was nine o'clock and time for everyone in Lollyland to release their stars.

I wish for my missing tiara to reappear, Itty thought.

She opened her hands and eyes and watched her star drift upward. Soon the night sky was filled with floating stars. It was the most beautiful thing Itty had ever seen, aside from the star shower the night before. But suddenly, something strange happened.

A huge gust of wind blew out of nowhere.

And it wasn't just one gust of wind. Suddenly it was really windy. Really, *really* windy.

Itty grabbed her dad's hand, worried she might blow away.

As the kingdom watched, all the stars swirled together and then shot up and away in a tangled ball of light.

Then the wind stopped as suddenly as it had started.

“Was that supposed to happen?” Itty asked.

The king smoothed his fur back into place, looking a little concerned. But then the look disappeared and he smiled. “I’m

sure it's nothing to worry about,"
he told Itty, patting her head.

Itty fell right to sleep that night. She knew the sooner she got to sleep, the quicker morning would come and she would have her tiara back.

As the sun hit her face the next morning, Itty smiled. She jumped out of bed and ran over to her closet. There, sitting on the center shelf, was her little pillow . . . with no tiara on it.

Itty peered behind piles of folded shirts. No tiara. She checked under her bed and behind her bookshelf. No tiara.

Itty decided to search the rest of the castle. Surely the tiara had to have been returned *somewhere.* She padded down the steps and saw Glenn in the grand hall with her parents. He was clutching his little red hat. He looked very worried.

"What's going on?" Itty asked.

Everyone turned to face her.

Why are they looking at me like that? Itty wondered.

Glenn coughed. "Um, Princess Itty . . . ," he began, squishing his hat into a ball. "Due to the unusual winds last night, the stars got mixed up."

"Mixed up?" Itty repeated. "What does that mean?"

"Well, it means that everyone's *wishes* got mixed up," the Queen responded.

"Mine too?" Itty squeaked.

The Queen gently put an arm around Itty's shoulders. "Darling, look in the mirror."

chapter 7

The Big Mix-Up

Itty had been staring at her reflection for five whole minutes. She looked from another angle. It was still there.

It was her tail, which was about twenty times longer than usual. It was so long that it wrapped itself in a coil and dragged behind her.

How did I not notice this when I woke up? Itty wondered. *And who in all of Lollyland wished for this?*

Itty unfurled her tail. It slid across the floor, reaching her parents and Glenn. She tried reeling it in, but it disobeyed, darting up and swatting Glenn.

"Sorry!" Itty cried. "I don't know how to control this thing!" Then Itty had an idea. "Mom, can I go

thwak

meet my friends?" she asked. She wondered what sort of mixed-up wishes *they* had been granted.

"Sure, sweetie," her mother replied. "We need to try and sort this out. And maybe one of *your* friends wished for that . . .

um . . . special tail and can help you with it."

Itty was pretty sure no one she knew had wished for a super-duper long tail. She was about to call a messenger fairy when there was a knock at the door.

Itty opened it and was surprised to see Luna, Esme, and Chipper.

"There's a TIGER living at my house!" Luna blurted out. "Oh Itty! Why is your tail SO long?!"

"Come in," Itty replied. "Just try not to yell because, you know, the glitter," she reminded her friend.

"Sorry! Why is your tail so long?" Luna whispered.

"Let's go have a snack and I'll tell you," Itty replied.

On their way to the kitchen Itty explained about the mixed-up wishes.

"Can it be fixed?" Luna asked.

"I like my tiger, but she belongs with whoever wished for her."

"That's how I feel about my lifetime supply of jelly beans!" Chipper exclaimed. "They look delicious, but they're all one flavor!"

"Strawberry, right?" Esme asked.

Chipper looked confused. "How did you know that?"

"I got the power of super-smell." Esme shrugged. "I can now smell things from a mile away. And speaking of smell, did someone bake confetti cookies? Yum!"

chapter 8

Wishes Gone Wrong

As the friends finished their snack, Esme said, "I wonder how Goodie Grove would smell to me now."

"Only one way to find out!" Itty exclaimed.

But just then the King entered the kitchen and shook his head.

"Things are very . . . confused outside, especially at Goodie Grove."

"From the mixed-up wishes?" Itty asked.

The King nodded. "Two young pigs were granted the ability to fly. Pigs are not meant to fly, of course, so they had some difficulty. They went to Goodie

Grove and knocked over the vats of syrup. As you can imagine, the syrup fairies were not happy."

Itty and her friends exchanged a look. Everyone knew better than to upset the syrup fairies.

OOF!

"Then there's the giraffe who woke up to find roller skates on his feet. As we know, giraffes can't skate! It's all very mixed up. But the Queen has dispatched announcement fairies. Everyone in the kingdom will gather, and we'll figure this out."

The King paused as his ears twitched. "It sounds like animals are starting to arrive. Itty, please be ready to join us on the balcony."

Itty's friends wished the King good luck and headed outside to find their families.

Itty went up to her bedroom. She knew that her tiara probably had not reappeared, but she had to check. Just in case.

The pillow was still empty.

As Itty turned to leave, she saw something out of the corner of her eye. It was her shooting star. And it was quivering. Almost as if it was *trying* to get Itty to notice it. Itty carefully removed the star from its display case.

Itty looked at her star. "What are you trying to tell me?" she asked. Then she shook her head. What was she doing talking to a star?

As Itty went to put her star back, she thought, *I just wish everyone in the kingdom would have their original wishes granted and we could get this all sorted out.*

Suddenly, the star glowed brighter than ever before. And then something even more amazing happened. The star floated from Itty's paws, through her open window, and then shot up into the sky.

Itty ran to the window and watched her star disappear.

Now she was a princess with no tiara *and* no shooting star.

chapter 9

The Second Shower

Itty rushed out to the balcony, where her parents were hearing the complaints of a very mixed-up kingdom.

"I never wished for an alarm clock!" crowed a rooster. "I wake up with the sun every morning!"

“What about my fur?” asked a lion, whose mane was so curly he could barely see out from it. “I look ridiculous!”

King Kitty raised his paws to address the crowd. “We are doing everything we can to fix this!”

The animals quieted, eager to hear what their king had to say.

Just then, Glenn ran onto the balcony. The King paused as Glenn whispered something in his ear.

"Really?" the King asked. Glenn nodded. The King then told the Queen, who addressed the crowd.

"We have just received word that *another* star shower is coming!" the Queen announced.

"A double star shower has never happened before in the history of Lollyland. It's due to begin any moment now, and you will be able to make your wish again."

The sky suddenly began to glow just as it had during the first star shower. And the stars began to fall. But *this* time, instead of scattering everywhere, the stars landed right in the paws and hands of the animals.

Itty watched as animals caught stars, made their wishes, and set their stars free. One by one, the stars gently drifted up to the sky.

Itty was so enchanted by what was happening that it took her a few minutes to realize she didn't have a star.

And then, just as the last star was released, Itty saw a bright ball of light coming toward her. She opened her hands and caught it.

It was a star.

And not just any star. It was her shooting star. It had come back to grant her wish.

chapter 10

Wishes Do Come True

When Itty woke up the next morning, the first thing she saw was her shooting star in its case, glowing softly. The next thing she saw—because she'd raced to her closet—was her tiara, right back where it belonged. She was so relieved.

And now she just hoped that *all* the mixed-up wishes had been fixed. There was only one way to find out! She dressed quickly and ran downstairs. She decided she'd first go to Luna's house to see if the tiger was still there.

As Itty reached the bottom of the stairs, she spotted glitter in the hallway.

Then she saw Luna, dressed in a beautiful gown made of flower petals.

"My wish came true!" Luna cried, twirling around.

“Luna, it’s so beautiful!” Itty exclaimed. “I love it! Does this mean that *everyone’s* wishes came true?”

“Mine did,” said Esme. She and Chipper were there too!

"I *can't* smell Luna's dress from a mile away, and I got the special butterfly bed I wished for!" Esme flitted her wings as Itty gave her an excited hug. "It's big enough to fit *both* my wings!"

"What about you, Chipper?" Itty asked.

"Allow me to demonstrate," Chipper replied. He took three short hops and then jumped all the way to the top of the staircase!

Itty, Esme, and Luna cheered.

"What about you, Itty?" Luna wondered. "Your tail is back to normal, but did your wish come true?"

"It sure did," Itty replied. Finally, she told her friends about the missing tiara. She still didn't know just where the tiara had gone, but she no longer cared. All that mattered was that it was back.

“We’re lucky that second star shower fixed everything,” Luna said.

Itty thought of her shooting star, glowing in her room. “I have a feeling it was more magic than luck,” she said with a wink.

Here's a sneak peek at Itty's next royal adventure!

Itty Bitty Princess Kitty, Luna Unicorn, Esme Butterfly, and Chipper Bunny were hanging out at one of their favorite spots in Lollyland: Mermaid Cove.

"I hope we see a mermaid today," Itty said. "I love hearing them sing."

"Me too," Esme agreed. "That's why this is the *best* place in Lollyland."

"What about Goodie Grove?" Chipper asked.

Goodie Grove was a hop, skip, and a jump from Mermaid Cove

and was *the* place to go for delicious treats.

"I don't think I could pick one favorite place," Itty said. "What about you, Luna?"

"Hmm . . ." Luna looked thoughtful. "Maybe it's someplace we haven't been yet, like Hot Chocolate Springs. My sister Stella's class went there last week!" A little bit of glitter spurted from Luna's horn, which always happened when she was excited. "I wish we could go!"